The
Tiara
Club

Emerald Ball

To Princess Esmee Rose, with love
VF
With special thanks to JD

www.tiaraclub.co.uk

ORCHARD BOOKS
338 Euston Road, London NW1 3BH
Orchard Books Australia
Level 17/207 Kent St, Sydney, NSW 2000

A Paperback Original
First published in Great Britain in 2008
Text copyright © Vivian French 2008
Cover illustration copyright © Sarah Gibb 2008
Inside illustrations copyright © Orchard Books 2008

The right of Vivian French to be identified as the author of this
work has been asserted by her in accordance with the Copyright,
Designs and Patents Act 1988.

A CIP catalogue record for this book is available
from the British Library.

ISBN 978 1 84616 881 9

1 3 5 7 9 10 8 6 4 2

Printed in Great Britain

Orchard Books is a division of Hachette Children's Books,
an Hachette Livre UK company

www.hachettelivre.co.uk

The Tiara Club

Emerald Ball

By Vivian French

ORCHARD BOOKS

The Royal Palace Academy
for the Preparation of Perfect Princesses

(Known to our students as "*The Princess Academy*")

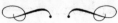

OUR SCHOOL MOTTO:
A Perfect Princess always thinks of others
before herself, and is kind, caring and truthful.

Emerald Castle offers a complete education for
Tiara Club princesses while taking full advantage of
our seaside situation. The curriculum includes:

A visit to Emerald Sea World Aquarium and Education Pool

Swimming lessons (safely supervised at all times)

A visit to Seabird Island

Whale watching

Our headteacher, Queen Gwendoline, is present at all
times, and students are well looked after by the school
Fairy Godmother, Fairy Angora.

Our resident staff and visiting experts include:

QUEEN MOLLY
(Sports and games)

KING JONATHAN
(Captain of the Royal Yacht)

LORD HENRY
(Natural History)

QUEEN MOTHER MATILDA
(Etiquette, Posture and Flower Arranging)

We award tiara points to encourage our Tiara Club princesses towards the next level. All princesses who win enough points at Emerald Castle will be presented with their Emerald Sashes and attend a celebration ball.

Emerald Sash Tiara Club princesses are invited to return to Diamond Turrets, our superb residence for Perfect Princesses, where they may continue their education at a higher level.

PLEASE NOTE:
Princesses are expected to arrive at the Academy with a *minimum* of:

TWENTY BALLGOWNS
(with all necessary hoops, petticoats, etc)

TWELVE DAY DRESSES

SEVEN GOWNS
suitable for garden parties, and other special day occasions

TWELVE TIARAS

DANCING SHOES
five pairs

VELVET SLIPPERS
three pairs

RIDING BOOTS
two pairs

Swimming costumes, playsuits, parasols, sun hats and other essential outdoor accessories as required

Hello there – I'm Princess Leah, and it's
SO lovely to know you're here with us!
Don't you just adore Emerald Castle?
We do. Oh! I'm so sorry! You do know
the rest of Daffodil Room, don't you?
Amelia, Ruby, Zoe, Millie and Rachel – they're
my special friends, just like you. Actually,
most people at Emerald Castle are very
nice – it's only Diamonde and Gruella who
are mean and nasty...you just never
know what they're going to do next!

Chapter One

"We know something you don't know! We know something you don't know!"

We did our best to ignore Diamonde as she minced her way past us, arm in arm with Gruella, but it wasn't easy. She was obviously DYING for us to ask her what she was talking about.

Once she reached the other side of the recreation room she made Gruella walk all the way back again, just so she could keep smiling her Know-It-All smile at us. In the end Millie couldn't bear it any longer.

"So what IS it you know and we don't?" she asked.

Diamonde smoothed her hair back, and tried to look superior. "That's for you to find out!" She gave a silly giggle, and nudged Gruella. "It's something very, very special, isn't it, Gruella? And WE'RE going to win!"

Gruella nodded. "We're going

to show Princess Beryl we're the best!"

"Who's Princess Beryl?" Ruby asked, but Diamonde shook her head. "It's a secret." And she giggled again and nudged Gruella in the most maddening way.

"Well," I said, "I don't really care about your secret. I'm going to go and have a paddle. Is anyone else coming?"

Of course Amelia, Rachel, Millie, Zoe and Ruby said they'd come with me, and we all trooped out together.

"Honestly!" Amelia exploded as we made our way out of Emerald Castle and down the steps to the sandy beach. "Those two are DREADFUL!"

"I know," Rachel agreed. "And I know we shouldn't take any notice when they go on like that, but I can't help wondering what their secret could be."

That made me laugh, because I'd been thinking exactly the same. "Let's have a look on the notice board when we go back into school," I suggested. "If anything interesting's going to happen, it'll be on there."

My friends all agreed, and we did
our best to forget about the twins
while we paddled about the rocks
looking for pretty shells and stones.

We were just wondering if we should go back and start getting ready for supper when we heard someone calling to us, and we saw Fairy G and Fairy Angora walking along the beach. Fairy G is our school fairy godmother and Fairy Angora's her assistant,

and they're both lovely, although Fairy G can be very scary when she's cross.

"Hello, princesses!" Fairy G said cheerfully. "Don't be late for supper! Dear Queen Gwendoline is going to make a really exciting announcement!"

"Something you'll just love," Fairy Angora added, and she smiled her beautiful smile.

We smiled back, and I don't know what made me say it, but I asked, "Is it something to do with Princess Beryl?"

Both fairy godmothers looked completely astonished. "However did you know that, Leah?" Fairy G sounded almost cross.

I gulped, and tried to think of some kind of explanation. It would have felt like telling tales to say the twins had been boasting about knowing a secret. "Erm... I heard someone mention her name," I said, and I knew it sounded feeble as I said it.

Fairy G gave me a thoughtful kind of stare. "Can you remember who that might have been, Leah?"

Before I could answer, Amelia said, "I think I heard her name somewhere as well, Fairy G," and Ruby, Rachel, Millie and Zoe nodded in agreement.

"I see." Fairy G was still looking thoughtful, but Fairy Angora smiled at us again. "Well, you'll soon know all about it! Hurry up and dry your feet, and we'll see you in the dining hall!"

Chapter Two

We did as we were told, and then set off to go back to school. Halfway there I noticed I'd left my towel behind, so I had to dash back to get it. I couldn't see it at first, so I climbed up one of the rocks so I could look round – and I suddenly realised Fairy G and Fairy Angora were standing talking immediately below me. I was about to call down, when I heard what Fairy G was saying...and I froze.

"I can't believe Leah would listen at a keyhole," she boomed.

"But we know SOMEONE was listening, because we both heard footsteps. And how did she know about Princess Beryl?"

Fairy Angora said something I couldn't hear, and Fairy G nodded. "Quite right. The best thing is to keep an eye on her. I'm afraid she can be quite deceitful."

I couldn't bear to listen any more. My face was absolutely burning as I crept down the rock, and fled back to school.

I felt completely sick as I rushed to catch up with my friends. If I hadn't actually heard Fairy G say what she did, I'd never have believed it. I'd always thought she really liked me – but obviously I was wrong.

"It's SO not fair!" I told myself angrily. "I'd NEVER listen at a door! And I'm NOT deceitful!" My head felt as if it was full of bumblebees. But then I thought, "Stop it, Leah! Just stay calm, and THINK..." And then I realised. It must have been the twins!

The twins must have been eavesdropping, and that was how they'd known about Princess Beryl! But it was me who was in trouble...

I took a deep breath, and walked

into school. I knew I couldn't tell tales, but I was determined to try and sort things out. "I'll talk to the twins," I decided. "Maybe if I tell them I know they've been listening at keyholes they'll own up to Fairy G..."

Even as I decided, I knew it wasn't likely the twins would ever admit to what they'd done. All the same, just trying would make me feel better.

Millie knew something was wrong as soon as I sat down next to her in the dining hall, but I didn't tell her what had happened. I just said I'd lost my towel. I'm sure she knew it was something more serious, but she didn't go on asking questions. The rest of our table were chatting about Queen Gwendoline's announcement, and I listened, but didn't say much.

Our head teacher has all kinds of lovely ideas for outings and trips to exciting places, although she's very strict about our manners, and the way we behave.

"Maybe it's another boat trip?" Zoe said hopefully. "Like when we went to Seabird Island."

"Or a trip to Emerald Sea World." Rachel winked at me. "You might see Prince Rosso again, Leah."

That took my mind off Fairy G for a moment, and I tried not to blush. I'd met Prince Rosso a couple of times, and I did think he was really nice – but I also knew he was nice to everyone, not just me.

"We'll soon find out what's going to happen," Amelia said. Here's Queen Gwendoline!"

We stood up and curtsied as Queen Gwendoline swept in and sailed up to the platform at the end of the hall, together with Fairy Angora and Fairy G.

"Princesses!" Queen Gwendoline began, and I noticed Diamonde

elbow Gruella. She saw me looking, and stuck her nose in the air, but I pretended I hadn't seen. I turned away, and watched as our head teacher pulled a big silver-edged card out of her handbag.

"You are very VERY fortunate," Queen Gwendoline went on. "I have an invitation from someone whom Fairy G and I have known for many years – Princess Beryl. Her father is King of Emerald Island, and she's asked you all to stay for a weekend to enjoy the many sporting facilities... And on the last night she's arranged a fabulous Emerald Ball."

She stopped for a moment, and there was the LOUDEST buzz of conversation. If the weather was very clear you could just about see Emerald Island on the other side of Emerald Bay, and we'd

often wondered about it. When we'd asked Queen Molly, our games teacher, she said she'd been there when she was a princess, and it was a kind of sports centre. It sounded SO exciting! She'd done archery, and ridden ponies, and practised rock climbing – but when we asked if we could go too she'd said no one was allowed there any more. It was very sad; apparently the old king who owned the island went away to live with his daughter somewhere else.

Queen Gwendoline held up her
hand, and the buzz died away.
"We are extremely grateful to
Princess Beryl," she went on. "She
has spent an enormous amount of
time and effort restoring the
island to its former glory." Our
head teacher paused, and smiled
at Fairy G. "Fairy G has already
been to the island, and she
and Fairy Angora have devised
a Magic Trail so you can have fun
finding out what's there. And now
I'll let Queen Molly give you the
details of the weekend..." Queen
Gwendoline looked round, and at
once the dining hall door opened,

and Queen Molly came bustling in
carrying a pile of paper.

"I'm so sorry I'm late," she puffed. "There's a message from Princess Beryl. She's arranged a special treat for the first princesses to complete Fairy G's Magic Trail. They'll fly in an air balloon to the Dancing Tower where the Emerald Ball will take place!"

Chapter Three

I don't think any of us took much notice of all the instructions Queen Molly gave us. We were MUCH too busy thinking about Emerald Island, and flying in an air balloon!

"Wouldn't it be GLORIOUS?" Zoe sighed as we finished our supper. "I've ALWAYS wanted to be able to fly."

"We'd see for miles and miles and MILES!" Ruby enthused.

"We'll have to try really hard to win the competition," Rachel said firmly.

Millie and Amelia nodded. "Daffodil Room for the air balloon ride!"

"That's what YOU think!" The twins were standing right behind us, and Diamonde was frowning. "YOU'RE not going to fly in the air balloon, you silly billy Daffodillies!"

"That's right." Gruella looked smug. "WE'RE going to win, so THERE!" She linked arms with her sister, and the two of them flounced off together. As they disappeared Amelia turned to me.

"What is it, Leah?" she asked. "You haven't said a word for ages and ages – and you're very pale. What's happened?"

Honestly – I nearly burst into tears. I really REALLY wanted to tell her, but I just couldn't. Instead I said, "I'll be all right soon. I...I've got something to sort out with the twins." And I got up and hurried after them.

I found them in the recreation room. They were studying a piece of paper, but as soon as they saw me Gruella sat on it.

"What do you want, Leah?" Diamonde asked rudely.

I took a deep breath. "I know you were listening outside Fairy G's room," I said. "Otherwise you wouldn't have known about Princess Beryl."

Gruella gave a little squeak, but Diamonde frowned. "SO WHAT?" she demanded. "What if we did hear? We were just walking past, and Fairy G's got the loudest voice ever."

"Well..." I hesitated. Diamonde was right about Fairy G's voice, and I didn't know whether to believe her or not. "Well...it's just that Fairy G thinks it was ME who overheard her."

Diamonde stared at me, and then began to smile. It wasn't a nice smile, and I suddenly wondered if I'd made a terrible mistake. "Well, well, well," she said. "Poor little Leah! But don't think I'M going to help you!" And she grabbed Gruella, snatched up the piece of paper, and marched off. I was left feeling silly...and wishing I hadn't said anything at all.

*

Soon afterwards it was time for bed, and the next day was SO busy I hardly had a moment to think about what had happened. We spent the morning packing our bags, and in the afternoon we were taken to the landing stage to wait for the Emerald Island boat to come and collect us. We found ourselves sitting next to the twins, and they spent the whole journey nudging each other, and whispering. Fairy G came and sat right behind us. I had a horrid feeling she was there so she could keep an eye on me, but

she seemed her usual jolly self and
I began to feel a bit better...until
we actually reached the island.

I was just about to follow the rest of Daffodil Room down the gangplank when Fairy G said, "Leah, dear – would you mind walking with me? I need someone sensible to help carry all my luggage."

My stomach did a somersault, and I picked up a couple of her bulging bags.

If I hadn't been feeling so mixed up inside, I'd have ADORED Emerald Island. Princess Beryl was SO welcoming, but she was older than I'd expected, and quite soon she said she was going to leave Fairy G in charge while she went to have a rest. Our room was fabulous, and from the window we could see ponies in a field, and a winding stream, and an adventure playground with a wonderful climbing tower. The twins were SO snooty about the tower; as we walked into the main hall of Emerald Island House Diamonde said in a loud whisper,

"Whoever heard of princesses having to climb a tower?"

Millie laughed. "In the old days princesses were always being shut up in towers. Just think of how much fun they'd have had if they'd been able to climb out!"

*

After supper we were sent to bed early. Fairy G said we would be starting on the Magic Trail just as soon we'd had breakfast the next day, so we'd need a good night's sleep.

"You'll have to have your wits about you," she said cheerfully. "We're going to give you a list of clues. If you get the answers right you'll have a lot of fun, even if you don't win."

"HURRAH!" Amelia looked excited. "I LOVE solving clues!"

Diamonde gave her a cold stare. "Well, you won't be as good as we are. Gruella and I are going to win. Just you wait and see!"

"That's right," Gruella agreed. "We're CERTAIN to win the balloon ride to the ball, aren't we, Diamonde?"

Fairy G didn't hear, because she'd gone to ring the bell – but it made me even more suspicious.

The twins MUST have heard more than just Princess Beryl's name...otherwise, how could Gruella be so sure they were going to win?

I'd thought I wouldn't be able to sleep that night, but I did – and I woke up to find the rest of Daffodil Room getting dressed.

"Come on, sleepy head!" Rachel smiled at me. "The Magic Trail's waiting!"

I jumped out of bed, and the six of us were the first downstairs. Fairy Angora handed us each a piece of paper as we went into the dining room, and while we ate our toast and marmalade we studied the clues.

"Begin by finding four legs, and look for the six in a ring," Rachel read out loud. "There you must leave four legs for two legs. Pick what is little, but will one day be big, and search for what always moves, but yet stays still.

Travel until you can go no further, and then remember Rapunzel. Where would you find her? Look carefully – and you may be rewarded!"

Millie clapped her hands. "Oh, I know! The ponies! We've got to find a pony to begin with!"

"What do you think the 'six in a ring?' could be?" Zoe asked.

I took off my spectacles, polished them, and put them back on again. It always helps me to think – and an idea was already buzzing in my head. "I'm sure I saw a stream from our bedroom window," I said, "and water moves but still stays in the same place. Shall I run upstairs and see if I can see the six in a ring anywhere near the stream?"

"That's BRILLIANT, Leah,"

Amelia told me, and I excused myself and hurried to our room.

As soon as I looked out of the window I knew what the answer was – there were six huge oak trees at the top of the hill.

"Hurrah!" I thought, and I was just about to run and tell the others when I heard a muffled sneeze. It seemed to be coming from the cupboard in the corner, and for just a second I felt cold all over. Suppose it was a burglar?

"Princess Leah, don't be such a coward!" I told myself. I opened the cupboard – and there were the twins!

Diamond was clutching a piece of paper, and they both looked SO astonished it was almost funny.

"WHATEVER are you doing?" I asked.

"That's exactly what I'D like to know!" said a booming voice from the doorway.

The twins came slowly out of the cupboard, and then, as they moved towards Fairy G, Diamonde scrumpled up the paper and dropped it.

"Please pick that up," Fairy G ordered, "and hand it to me."

Diamonde's face went bright red, but she left the paper where it was.

"It's only rubbish," she said. "We...we found it on the floor in here. We thought we'd tidy it up."

Fairy G strode forward, and picked up the paper herself. She smoothed it out, and read it.

"'Ponies... Trees on the hill...' I see." Fairy G sounded VERY grim. "The answers to the competition."

"OH!" Diamonde gave a little scream, and pointed at me. "LEAH! How could you!" She swung round to Fairy G. "Leah must have been listening outside your study when you were making up the clues with Fairy Angora! That's TERRIBLE!"

60

Fairy G grew to about twice her usual height, folded her arms, and glared at Diamonde. "And how, Diamonde, do you know Fairy Angora and I made up the clues in my study?"

Diamonde opened and shut her

mouth, and went deadly pale.
There was an icy silence...and then
Gruella stepped forward.

"We heard you," she said.
"I told Diamonde we shouldn't
listen, but...but we sort of couldn't
help it. We're VERY sorry..."

Fairy G was still glaring at Diamonde. "And why were you in the cupboard? Could it be that you were hoping to get Daffodil Room into trouble by leaving the answers here for me to find?"

Diamonde hung her head. "Sort of..." she muttered. "I knew you thought Leah had been eavesdropping...and...and I was worried Daffodil Room would win the competition..."

"WHAT?" Fairy G's bellow was so loud the windows rattled. "I would NEVER believe that of Leah, but I'm afraid I've always suspected you were deceitful, Diamonde. I've even told Fairy Angora so, and we've both been keeping an eye on you ever since we heard you whispering outside my study. Sadly, it seems we were right.

Now, please go and wait for me downstairs. You will NOT be allowed to enter the competition, and I very much doubt if Queen Gwendoline will allow you to attend the ball tomorrow!"

As the twins trailed dismally

away, Fairy G turned to me. "Hadn't you better hurry?" she asked, and her eyes were twinkling. "The rest of Daffodil Room are longing to get out on the Magic Trail, and they won't go without you!"

"Thank you!" I said, and I couldn't help giving Fairy G the most enormous hug – I was SO relieved everything had been sorted out. She looked surprised, but pleased – and then I absolutely ZOOMED down the stairs. My friends were waiting for me...

And off we went!

Chapter Six

Did we win the competition? We did! We got ALL the clues right, and we were the first to reach the top of the climbing tower. We looked round, hardly daring to breathe, and then Rachel gave a sudden excited squeak.

"Look!" she said, and pointed.

Propped against the wall was a golden envelope, and inside was a sparkly ticket that said:

WELL DONE!
YOU WILL RIDE IN
THE SILVER BALLOON TO
THE DANCING TOWER!

We were SO thrilled we actually screamed, and we danced up and down for AGES. We couldn't believe it – we'd really, really won!

The following evening we got
dressed in our special ball gowns,
and it was SUCH fun. We were all
wearing green because it was the
Emerald Ball, and my dress was

the most beautiful shimmery green silk. Amelia's was gorgeous as well, and she had a pink bangle, and I had a pink fan – and we hadn't planned it at all!

When we were ready we hurried outside, and there – outside Emerald Island House – was the most BEAUTIFUL balloon. We climbed in, and the balloon master saluted us. "To the Dancing Tower!" he said. The pages let go of the ropes, and up, up we flew...

Good day to you, princess.
'Tis Princess Amelia, who brings you
greetings from all in Daffodil Room at
Emerald Castle. The noble princesses
Leah, Millie, Zoe, Ruby and Rachel
join me in wishing you well...
Oh, it's no good. I just CAN'T
write like a Perfect Princess!
But I know you won't mind
because you're our friend...

Chapter One

I don't think I've ever been so thrilled as I was when we floated to the Dancing Tower in our air balloon. I'd been a teensy bit nervous before we started, but the balloon master was so nice I soon felt fine. And besides, I did have all the rest of Daffodil Room with me. Ruby and Millie held hands very tightly as we took off, so I guessed they were a bit anxious as well – but as soon as we were up in the air we enjoyed every single second. We could see for MILES! We could see our school, Emerald Castle, on the other side

of the bay, and Seabird Island, and the whole of Emerald Island spread out below us like a map. We could even see the coaches taking the rest of our friends to the Dancing Tower, and it felt amazing to be flying high above them.

"Hey!" Millie suddenly leant right out of the basket. "I can see a boat heading for Emerald Island, and it looks as if there are LOADS of people on board – who do you think they can be?"

"That'll be the princes from the Princes Academy, Your Highness," the balloon master told her. "On their way to the ball, they are." His eyes twinkled. "Might you be looking forward to seeing anyone in particular?"

Millie shook her head. "I just hope they're fun to dance with," she said, "and that they don't tread on my toes."

Ruby gave Leah a tiny nudge. "Do you think Prince Rosso will be there?" she asked. Leah did her best to look as if she didn't know what Ruby was talking about, and Rachel smiled. "It's OK, Leah," she said. "We all thought he was nice, but he did seem to really like you."

83

"What about Prince Wincey?" Zoe began to giggle. "He dances like a bouncing ball!"

That made us laugh, although I felt a little bit mean... Why?

I'll tell you a secret.

I was really really hoping Prince Wincey would be at the Emerald Ball, and that he'd ask me to dance. We'd met him when we were studying sealife in the aquarium, and he did talk in the weirdest way – but he was SUCH fun! I hadn't said anything to my friends though. I didn't want them to feel sorry for me if he danced with someone else all evening.

Chapter Two

I found myself holding my breath as the balloon master brought the balloon gently down to land on the tower, but there wasn't even the slightest bump.

"Here we are at last, Your Highnesses," he said with a bow. "Safe and sound on the top of Dancing Tower!"

"Thank you SO much!" Rachel gave him a dazzling smile. "That was MAGIC!"

And I know we all agreed with her. There we were, in our very, VERY best ballgowns, arriving at the Emerald Ball in SUCH style...

And as the basket settled a fanfare
of trumpets sounded and a page
came marching over to bow and
show us the way.

"Welcome to the Emerald Ball,"
he declared.

"Thank you so much," we said, and we smoothed our hair and shook out our dresses as we walked out onto a wonderfully silvery ballroom floor. Princess Beryl was sitting on a gorgeous throne surrounded by swathes of pretty green net studded with sparkling emeralds, and she stood up to greet us as we walked towards her.

"Welcome, my dears! And I do hope you enjoy yourselves this evening."

"Thank you, Your Majesty," I said as we curtsied very low. "I'm sure we will."

Princess Beryl smiled at us. "Excellent! And now I have a favour to ask. My little niece is staying here on the island with me, and she begged and begged me to let her come to the ball – would you mind looking after her? Fairy G tells me you are all very kind."

We curtsied again. "It would be our pleasure," Ruby told her.

"Thank you!" Princess Beryl looked pleased. "Now, I asked the balloon master to make sure you arrived a little early so you could meet her before the other princes and princesses arrive..."

She turned, and beckoned, and the door at the end of the tower opened. At once a small girl dressed in the prettiest little frock rushed towards us, and threw herself at her aunt, Princess Beryl.

"Auntie!" she squeaked. "I want

to DANCE! Make the musicians play THIS MINUTE!"

"They'll play very, very soon, Lillibelle," Princess Beryl soothed her. "Now, I want you to meet these lovely princesses. They're going to look after you, and make sure you have a lovely time."

Lillibelle jumped round, and stared at us. "But I don't WANT to be looked after by them! You said YOU'D dance with me, Auntie Beryl."

"I know I promised, Lillibelle, dear," Princess Beryl explained, "but I'm going to be very busy this evening."

Her little niece stamped her foot. "You promised! You promised! I don't want those horrid girls!" And she flung herself on the floor in a massive temper tantrum.

I don't think any of us knew quite what to do. I couldn't help thinking Princess Beryl shouldn't

have promised; Fairy G was always
telling us, "A Perfect Princess
Always Keeps Her Promises." It
would have been horribly rude to
say anything, though.

Princess Beryl gave a sigh, and said, "Lillibelle's SO overexcited. Perhaps you could take her to the supper room, and find her some cake?"

We didn't have time to answer, because Lillibelle was back on her feet and dancing round and round us. "YES!" she said, and she grabbed my hand. "I want some cake NOW! What's your name?"

"Amelia," I told her.

"Come on, 'Melia." Lillibelle tugged me towards the door. "Hurry up!" She gave my friends an imperious stare. "You can come too, if you like."

Leah, Ruby, Zoe, Rachel and Millie followed as Lillibelle pulled me down the tower stairs and into the supper room.

It was beautifully decorated, and the tables of food looked delicious, but I don't think any of us took a great deal of notice. We were hurrying after Lillibelle as she flew towards a table heaped with hundreds of different kinds of cake and jellies and cream.

"Will we be looking after her ALL the time, do you think?" Millie whispered anxiously as the little girl stopped to inspect the cakes.

"We won't be able to do much dancing," Zoe whispered back.

I leapt forward to save a massive chocolate gateau from toppling to the floor as Lillibelle pulled at the tablecloth. "Lillibelle, shall I put some on a plate for you?" I suggested.

Lillibelle stuck out her lower lip. "But I want to do it myself!"

"But you're wearing a VERY pretty party dress," Rachel said cunningly, "and you don't want to get it messy. Why don't you let Amelia do it?"

Lillibelle actually smiled, and she suddenly looked quite pretty. "All right."

"That was clever of you," I said as Rachel handed me a knife.

Rachel grinned. "I've got two little sisters, and they can be dreadful...but I've got an idea."

"What's that?" Millie asked.

"Why don't we take it in turns to look after her? If we split up, and three of us dance while the other three look after Lillibelle we can still have a fabulous—"

"NO!" Lillibelle had overheard Rachel, and she was glowering at her. "I only want 'MELIA! If she doesn't look after me I'll tell Auntie Beryl you're all HORRIBLE and then she'll be very, very, very, VERY cross!"

"Uh uh," Ruby said. "'A Perfect Princess always thinks of others before herself.' Looks like we're going to get some good practice."

I handed Lillibelle the plate of cake while I tried to think of a way to persuade her to let us dance. "I think Lillibelle really likes dancing. Maybe she could dance with each of us in turn, and see who's the best?"

A Perfect Princess should never boast, but I did think I'd made a really good suggestion – and Lillibelle beamed at me.

"NICE 'Melia," she said, and I thought, "Hurrah! I've done it!"

But then she went on, "I'll dance with you, but I don't want the others. Let's go NOW!" And she jumped up so quickly she tipped the plate over...and creamy chocolate gateau slid all down the front of my very best ballgown.

Chapter Three

To be fair, Lillibelle did look very sorry that she'd spoiled my dress. She snatched a napkin off the table and started scrubbing at the stain – and that made it look SO much worse! I could feel tears welling up in my eyes, but I blinked them away.

"Don't worry, Lillibelle," I said.

"I'll try and find a wet cloth..."

"Poor 'Melia," she said sadly. "You look ever so messy. None of the boy princes will dance with you now."

I had a dreadful feeling she was right, but Millie slipped off her soft green shawl. "Here," she said, and she draped it over the dirty marks so it looked like an overskirt. "That'll hide the worst of it."

"That's pretty," Lillibelle said approvingly, and then, "Hurry up! You said we were going to dance!"

I gave Millie a hug. "You're SO kind. Are you sure?"

"Quite sure. It's really warm tonight." Millie squeezed my hand. "And we're going to have a WONDERFUL time!"

"Me too," Lillibelle chipped in. "Come and dance!"

By the time we'd climbed back up the stairs and walked out onto the dance floor, all our friends had arrived, and the princes too. The musicians were tuning up,

and Princess Beryl was floating about making everybody welcome. I saw Fairy G and Fairy Angora chatting in a corner and I wanted to go and ask them what to do about my dress, but Lillibelle wouldn't let me.

"You've got to stay HERE," she complained, and her lower lip began to tremble. I was scared she might have another temper tantrum, so I stayed where I was, and waited for the music to begin.

As soon as it did a really handsome prince came hurrying across the dance floor and bowed to me.

"Excuse me," he said, "but would you care to dance?"

Before I could answer, Lillibelle grabbed my hand. "She's not dancing," she told the prince. "She's here to look after ME! Aren't you, 'Melia?"

What could I say? "A Perfect Princess always puts the wishes of others before her own"...and I was beginning to feel more and more sorry for Lillibelle. Princess Beryl wasn't taking any notice of her at all, and there weren't any other children her age for her to play with. I did my best to look cheerful, and said, "Thank you so much for asking me...but I'm going to dance with Lillibelle."

The prince gave me a rather chilly bow and moved away, and a moment later I saw him dancing with Princess Katie from Rose Room. Lillibelle gave me a huge smile.

"You're REALLY nice, 'Melia," she said. "Auntie Beryl said she'd dance with me yesterday, but today she said she was too busy. Can we dance now?"

I took her hands, and we whirled away into the polka.

Lillibelle was as light as a feather, and we whizzed round and round until we were dizzy, and then collapsed onto a bench. All the rest of Daffodil Room were dancing, and I was pleased to see Leah was chatting away to Prince Rosso – they seemed to be getting on brilliantly. I couldn't see Prince Wincey anywhere, though, and I began to wonder if he hadn't been invited.

Lillibelle pulled at my arm. "I want a drink, 'Melia. Can we go and find a drink? Please?"

"OK," I said, and I got up. Lillibelle put her hand in mine, and we walked away to the stairs leading to the supper room. We found some lemonade, and I made her sit on a chair while she drank it, and she was as good as gold.

"What would you like to do now?" I asked her.

Lillibelle's eyes sparkled. "Can I have some ice cream? Strawberry ice cream?"

"If you stay sitting on your chair," I promised, "I'll fetch you some."

She sat right back on her chair, and I went to fetch the ice cream, but just as I was spooning it into a bowl she bobbed up beside me. "I want to get some for you, 'Melia," she said, "because you're my friend and you're nice to me." And before I could stop her she'd grabbed an enormous serving spoon, scooped up a HUGE dollop of strawberry ice cream, wobbled – and dropped it all over my pretty dancing shoes.

"Oh NO!" Lillibelle squeaked. "I didn't mean to! I didn't mean to!" She burst into floods of tears and flung her arms round me.

"It's all right," I said, "really it is—" And that's when I realised she was still holding the serving spoon. As well as chocolate cake I now had strawberry ice cream all over my dress, and there was no way Millie's wrap could hide it. On top of everything else Lillibelle was covered as well, and I could feel melting ice cream sliding between my toes...

"Oh NO," I thought. "Things just CAN'T get any worse!"

Then I looked up, and saw Prince Wincey walking towards me across the supper room.

Chapter Four

I don't think I've ever seen anyone look so surprised. His eyes almost popped out of his head as he stared at me, and he gave a kind of gulp.

"Oh – I say! Bit of a mess, what. I say, old bean – we can't have that, you know. Not at all—" And before I could say a word he'd turned round and rushed away.

I SO nearly burst into tears myself. If Lillibelle hadn't been hiding her grubby little face in my chest I think I would have done, but I wanted to make her feel better. She seemed genuinely upset, and I knew she'd only been trying to do something nice for me...it wasn't her fault it had all gone so terribly wrong.

"Don't cry," I whispered in her ear. "We'll get you cleaned up, and then we'll go and have another dance, shall we?"

She wiped her nose with her fist, and nodded. I looked round to see where the bathrooms were, and we spent the next fifteen minutes washing her face and hands, and getting the worst of the ice cream off her dress and my dress and shoes...and I finally made her laugh by wriggling my toes at her.

"Maybe the ice cream will make me a better dancer," I told her, and she giggled as we went back to the supper room. Luckily, it was still empty. I knew I still looked a complete mess, so I suggested

we had a little dance there...but Lillibelle had other ideas.

"You're the best dancer ever, 'Melia," she told me. "Come and dance properly! And..." she gave me a sweet little sideways smile, "if you want to dance with a handsome boy prince, I'll let you."

"It's OK," I said. "I'm very happy dancing with you."

She sighed, and leant against me. "You're LOVELY. I wish you were my big sister. My big brother plays with me sometimes, but he's not nearly as nice as you."

I gave her a hug, and we went back to the dance floor. The music had stopped, and Princess Beryl was making a speech telling everyone where the supper room was, and how she hoped we were all having a lovely time. Lillibelle

and I slipped behind Rachel and Leah, and I noticed Leah was standing VERY close to Prince Rosso...but I couldn't see any sign of Prince Wincey.

Princess Beryl finished her speech
by saying she would lead everyone
down to supper, and there was
a burst of applause. She curtsied,
and swept towards the door
Lillibelle and I had just come out
of…and that's when she saw us.

"Oh my GOODNESS!" she gasped as she stared at our dresses. "What HAVE you both been doing? I really thought you were a responsible girl, Princess Amelia – but just LOOK at you! And little Lillibelle too! I am shocked! DEEPLY shocked! How COULD you get in such a state?"

I couldn't say a word. My stomach felt colder than the ice cream, and my heart was pounding. The princess's eyes were flashing, and she looked really angry – but then a voice spoke from behind her.

"I say, Ma'am – that's not fair. Not fair at all! The poor old thing was doing a great job of looking after little Trouble there – saw it for myself. Didn't say a word when Trouble tipped ice cream all over her shoes! Splendid stuff. Perfect Princess, if ever I saw one!" Prince Wincey stepped forward, and bowed as he handed me a beautiful satin cloak. "Best I could do, old bean. Cover the mess up, what!"

As Prince Wincey arranged the cloak around my shoulders, Lillibelle jumped forwards and tugged at her aunt's hand.

"My 'Melia's LOVELY!" she declared. "Don't say horrid things about her, Auntie Beryl! 'Melia promises me things, and she always, always does them – not like you! It was me that spilt the cake and ice cream and I LOVE 'Melia!"

It was Princess Beryl's turn not to be able to say a word. She looked at Prince Wincey, and she stared at Lillibelle, and then she looked at me again.

"It seems," she said at last, "that I've made a mistake. Princess Amelia, I ask your pardon!"

I could feel myself going bright

red. "Er..." I stuttered. "That is...thank you very much, Your Highness..."

And then there was one of those horrid embarrassing silences, until—

"What's all this?" Fairy G's

familiar boom echoed round the dance floor, and she strode forwards. "Goodness me, Amelia! Have you been rolling in chocolate cake and ice cream? And the little girl? Is this your niece, Princess Beryl?"

Princess Beryl nodded. "Princess Amelia was taking care of her for me," she explained. "It...it seems there was an accident. But it wasn't Amelia's fault," she added hastily as both Prince Wincey and Lillibelle glared fiercely at her.

"Hmph." Fairy G gave me a beaming smile, and the teeniest wink. "Time for a little magic, I'd say..." And she waved her wand.

*

Have you ever watched snow melting in the sunshine? Well, the stains on my dress and Lillibelle's frock melted away just the same, until we both looked as good as new...and my shoes did, too.

I no longer needed Prince Wincey's cloak! Lillibelle did a twirl, and crowed with delight. "My dress is all pretty again! Thank you! Thank you very much!" And she curtsied to Fairy G.

"I see you've been taking lessons from Amelia," Fairy G told her with a twinkle in her eye.

"Quite right too," Prince Wincey said, and he turned to me with a bow. "Might I offer to escort you to the supper room, old bean? And to take a spin on the dance floor afterwards?"

I hesitated. "I'd love to," I said, and I really meant it. "But...but I did promise Lillibelle I'd look after her."

"No problem!" Wincey grinned at Lillibelle. "We'll dance all three of us together!"

I couldn't help giving him the most enormous smile. He was SO kind – but Fairy G shook her head.

"This little one should be in

bed," she said firmly. "She's had a lovely time, but she's getting tired. I'll look after her now, Amelia. Perfect Princesses deserve to have fun!"

I looked at Lillibelle to see what she thought, but she was beaming happily at Fairy G. "Will you tell me a fairy story?" she asked.

"Maybe she'll tell you a story about a Perfect Princess called Amelia!" Wincey suggested as he took my arm. "Night night, little Lillibelle!"

"Night night," she said sleepily, and she blew me a kiss. "Night night, lovely 'Melia..."

Did I enjoy the rest of the Emerald Ball?

What do you think?

I had a FABULOUS time...and so did all my friends. We danced and danced and DANCED, and Wincey made me laugh more than anyone I've ever met.

He insisted on dancing with each of my friends in turn, but then he came back to dance with me...and at the end of the Emerald Ball he actually kissed my hand.

As the coaches took us back to Emerald Island House I felt SO happy...and I know all my friends did, too.

"What an absolutely magical evening," Leah said as we rattled up to the front door.

"Magical for you...and us...and even more magical for Amelia," Ruby said, and we smiled at each other.

Do you know what?

I can't wait until the next time when we're all together...

And DO make sure you're there too.

Friends for ever!

Tiara Club for ever!

Don't miss  website at:

www.tiaraclub.co.uk

Keep up to date with the latest
Tiara Club books and meet all
your favourite princesses!

There is SO much to see and do,
including games and activities. You can
even become an exclusive member of the
Tiara Club Princess Academy.

PLUS, there's exciting
competitions with
WONDERFUL prizes!

Be a Perfect Princess – check it out today!

This Christmas, look out for

Midnight Masquerade

with Princess Emma & Princess Jasmine

Hello...this is Princess Emma.
I'm so very VERY glad you're there,
because I've never been to a boarding
school before...have you? I'd read
a lot of books, and it sounded
fun - but only if you have loads and
loads of friends. And before I went
to the Princess Academy I didn't
have many friends...

When my mum and dad announced that they were going on an extra long Royal Tour, I was thrilled. I've always gone with them, ever since I was tiny – and it's fun! Of course you have to do lots of waving at people, and smile until your cheeks are really REALLY sore – but I've never minded doing that.

Does that make me sound like a show-off? I didn't ever think of it that way. It was just something I did because my mum and dad told me to...and (here's the secret bit I don't tell most people) it meant I could stay with them, instead of having to stay at home. I HATE being at home without them. (You won't tell anyone, will you?) So when Mum said something about staying with Aunt Alice for part of the Royal Tour I said, "Ooooh! That'll be fun!"

And then it happened. Mum gave me surprised look and said, "Oh, Emma! Didn't your father tell you? You're not coming with us this time. You're going to go to school."

I burst into tears, even though we were just outside the stables, and the stable boy was looking at me. I SO didn't want to be sent away!

Oh dear. You'll think I'm a terrible baby – but I promised myself I'd tell the truth, because a Perfect Princess always does.

Anyway, I burst into tears, and Mum gave me a hug. She said she was really sorry – Dad was supposed to have told me the day before.

"I don't have to go, do I?" I sniffed. "I want to go with you and Dad, like always."

Mum shook her head. "I'm sorry, darling. It's all arranged. The Princess Academy is where

I went when I was your age, and I LOVED it." A wistful look came over her face. "It was the happiest time of my life. I made SO many friends while I was there, and you will too."

I didn't think she was right, but I couldn't say so. If I'd said anything else I'd have started crying again, and the stable boy was staring at me. Even my pony was giving me a disapproving look.

Mum took my hand. "Come along," she said. "I've got all the details in my office. I'll show you the prospectus – and there's a letter there from my dear friend

Queen Tallulah. Her daughter's going to the Academy tomorrow as well, and we've arranged for the two of you to travel together. Isn't that lovely? You'll arrive with a friend, so you'll be just fine!"

I hardly heard what Mum was saying about friends. I'd heard the word *tomorrow* – and I could hardly breathe.

"T...T...TOMORROW?" I gasped. "I've got to go TOMORROW?"

Mum nodded. "Didn't I say? Mrs Stacey's up in your room now, packing your trunk. SUCH a good thing we bought you those new ballgowns! You'll look SO sweet at the Midnight Masquerade."

"What Midnight Masquerade?" I was beginning to wonder if I was fast asleep and having a horrible nightmare.

"There's always a ball during the Christmas term," Mum told me. "And this year it's extra special. The princes from the Princes' Academy will be there, and you'll all be wearing masks until midnight." And she actually did a little spin in the middle of the stable yard! The little stable boy's eyes opened VERY wide, and my pony whinnied in surprise.

Before I could say anything else
Mum hurried me away to our
palace...
And I felt more and MORE as if
it was all a terrible dream.

~ *Want to read more?* ~
Midnight Masquerade with Princess Emma
& Princess Jasmine is out in October 2008!